Spider's Big Match

Written by Alan Durant

Illustrated by Philip Hopman

Collins

CHAPTER 1

Spider McDrew was a hopeless case. Everyone said so.
His mother said it each morning when Spider came down
to breakfast wearing one blue sock and one orange sock,
or with his jumper on back to front.

"Oh, Spider," she said, shaking her head sadly,
"you're a hopeless case."

Mr Smithers, his teacher at Parkfield School, said it too, whenever he asked Spider a question and got the wrong answer.

"What's five times six, Spider?"
"Ninety-four million, sir."
"What's the capital of France, Spider?"
"The Atlantic Ocean, sir."
"Spider McDrew, you're a hopeless case."

It wasn't that Spider was stupid. He knew that five times six is thirty. He knew that the capital of France is Paris. It was just that his mind wandered and he was always one step behind everyone else.

One moment he was sitting listening to Mr Smithers, and then it was as if a bee came buzzing by and suddenly he was thinking about something else completely. The answers he gave were to questions that Mr Smithers had asked a long time before. How many miles is the sun from the Earth? What ocean separates Europe from America?

The children in his class thought Spider was hopeless too. He was always messing up their playground games.

"You're it, Spider," said Darren Kelly, when they were playing tag.
Spider frowned. Then he took a step forward.
"What's the time, Mr Wolf?" he cried.
The other children groaned.
"We're not playing that game any more, Spider," said Jason Best.
"You're hopeless, Spider," said Kip Keen.

The children didn't ask Spider to play any more.
At breaktime, he just wandered round the playground,
in a world of his own, daydreaming. He looked a real
sight too. His clothes were a mess, his shoes were
scuffed and his coal-black hair sprouted wildly from his
head like the leaves of a spider plant. That's why his
nickname was Spider. His real name was Spencer, but
hardly anybody called him that. Even his mother called
him Spider most of the time. He was Spider McDrew,
the hopeless case.

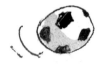

CHAPTER 2

Parkfield was only a small village school, but it had a very good football team. In fact, with just one match left to play, Parkfield was top of the league.

"All we need is to draw our last game against Stoneley and we'll be champions," Mr Smithers told his team. "But if Stoneley win, then they'll be champions." It was a very important match.

"Don't worry, sir, we'll win," said Neil "Deadeye" Phillips, Parkfield's ace striker and captain.
"Yeah, we'll destroy them," snarled Darren Kelly.
He punched the air and made loud, destroying noises.
"Darren," said Mr Smithers, "it's a football match, not World War Three."

Everyone was excited about the match – even girls like Emma Flowers and Hannah Stewart, who hated football.

"I'm sure we'll win – and so's Barbie," said Hannah Stewart. Barbie was Hannah Stewart's favourite toy. "Snuggles is sure we'll win too. He says we'll win four love," said Emma Flowers. Snuggles was Emma Flowers's new pet, a golden brown and white guinea pig which she loved very much.

Spider was very excited about the match too, even though he wasn't in the team.

Then, the day before the match, disaster struck.
Chickenpox hit Parkfield! One by one, the football team
broke out in rashes and spots: Kip Keen, Matthew Jones,
Verbushan Patel, Neil Phillips ...
As each was sent home, Mr Smithers
had to call up a reserve to take
his place. But by the end of
the afternoon, Mr Smithers
still needed one more player.

"My brother's brilliant," Darren
Kelly suggested. "He's top scorer
for his school."

"That's very good, Darren," said Mr Smithers. "But we
can only choose children who go to Parkfield. I think
your brother's a bit old for our team, too, don't you?"
Darren Kelly's brother was fourteen.

"We could play a man short," said
Jason Best, who was the team
captain now that Neil Phillips had
chickenpox. "Teams play better with
only ten men. Gary Lineker said so."

10

"Mmm," said Mr Smithers. "That's very interesting, Jason, but I think we have to start the match with a full team." He looked round the class with a heavy heart. He had no choice: Spider would have to play.

Spider was delighted. He smiled like he'd never smiled before. "I won't let you down, sir," he said. "I'll ... "
But what he would do no one ever knew, for at that moment, his mind wandered.
Mr Smithers shrugged his shoulders and sighed.

CHAPTER 3

On the way home, Spider happily kicked stones along
the pavement. He was in the football team – he, Spider
McDrew! He jumped and waved his arms in the air as
he'd seen Neil Phillips do when he
scored a goal. Then, bump,
he slipped on some wet
leaves and fell on his bottom.
At the same time, his mind
wandered from football
to nature.

"I wonder if leaves have feelings?" he thought,
as he picked himself up. He was very careful not to
tread on any, just in case.

Spider was almost home when he saw a ball on the path in front of him. Without thinking, he kicked at it. He aimed a straight kick, but instead he kicked across the ball. He watched in surprise as the ball curved away like a banana. Through the air it soared, across the road and ... wham! Straight into his mother's best potted geranium!

Crash! Smash! The flowerpot tipped over and broke on the concrete path. The front door opened and his mum appeared. She looked very angry.

"Spider!" she cried. "Whatever do you think you're doing?"

Spider was very sorry. He helped his mum pick up the pieces of broken flowerpot and tried to explain what had happened. Luckily, the geranium wasn't damaged. His mum scooped it up gently and put it into another pot.

"You really must be more careful, Spider," she said.
"If you want to play football, go to the park."

"Yes, Mum," said Spider. Then he remembered about
the big match.
"Mum," he said, "I'm in the football team!"
Spider's mum could hardly believe her ears.
She nearly dropped the new flowerpot.
"That's wonderful," she said.
Spider told his mum the whole story.

"It's lucky you've had chickenpox," she said.
"Will you come and watch me play?" Spider asked.
"I wouldn't miss it for the world," said Spider's mum.
She gave Spider a kiss. "I'll leave work early. But I
might not be there for the start."
"That's OK. Thanks, Mum," said Spider happily.
Spider's mum ruffled his hair so that it looked even
more sprouty than usual. "I'll expect you to score a
goal, of course," she said. "Spider. Spider?"

Spider looked at her blankly. He wasn't thinking
about football any more.

"Mum, do leaves have feelings?" he asked.

Spider's mum shook her head and smiled.

"You're a hopeless case, Spider McDrew!"
she laughed.

CHAPTER 4

The next afternoon, when Spider stood waiting for the kick-off, he felt very nervous. He so wanted to do well that his stomach was a-flutter with butterflies. Lots of parents had come to see the match, but Spider couldn't see his mum.

"Come on, Stoneley!" shouted the Stoneley parents.
"Come on, Parkfield!" shouted the Parkfield parents.
Mr Smithers blew his whistle. The game was on!

For most of the first half, Stoneley were on the attack.
The play was all in the Parkfield half and Spider hardly
got a kick. He watched as a Stoneley striker hit a terrific
shot that soared towards the top corner of the net.
It looked like a goal all the way. But no, the Parkfield
goalkeeper, Jack Smith, sprang like a cat through the air
and turned the ball around the post.

"Great save!" the crowd cried.

Jason Best waved at Spider.

"Everyone back for the corner," he called.

"Come on, Spider!" shouted Darren Kelly. Spider ran
back quickly.

"Stand in the goalmouth by that post, Spider,"
Jason ordered.

The corner came over. The Stoneley striker rose highest
and headed the ball. It looped across the goal, over the
hands of Jack Smith, towards Spider on the goal line.

"Get it away, Spider!" his team-mates shouted.
But Spider was still thinking about Jack Smith's
brilliant save and instead of heading the ball he
dived and pushed it round the post with his hand.

"Penalty!"

Mr Smithers blew his whistle and pointed to the penalty spot.

The Stoneley striker stepped forward and wham, the ball flew into the Parkfield net! Stoneley were in the lead! The Stoneley players and supporters jumped for joy. The Parkfield players and supporters groaned.

Spider hung his head in shame. He'd let the whole school down. He was glad his mum hadn't arrived. When the half-time whistle blew, he just wanted to run away and hide. But Mr Smithers called the whole team around him and gave them a stern talking to.

"You're giving the ball away too much," he said. "You've got to think more and try harder."

Spider waited for his teacher to tell him he was a hopeless case for what he'd done. But Mr Smithers didn't say anything about the penalty. As the players lined up for the second-half kick-off, he put his hand on Spider's shoulder. "Don't let your head drop, lad," he said quietly. "Just do your best."

Those few, kind words had a big affect on Spider. He went out for the second half with new heart and determination.

CHAPTER 5

Straight from the kick-off, Parkfield went on the attack. They passed the ball around carefully, waiting for an opening. Spider played his part, running hard and not giving the ball away once. Parkfield got a corner and another one ... they had lots of shots. They hit the bar and the post. But still a goal would not come. Then, with ten minutes left, Jason Best burst through the Stoneley defence and, as the goalkeeper came out, he chipped the ball beautifully ... just over the bar.

"Great try!" shouted the Parkfield crowd.

The next time Spider got the
ball, he kept it instead of
passing. He turned past one
defender ...

... nutmegged a second,
pushing the ball between
his legs ...

... and skipped over the tackle
of a third.

The Parkfield crowd bayed with excitement as Spider swerved past the last defender and sent the Stoneley goalkeeper tumbling into the mud.

The goal was at Spider's mercy. No one could catch him.

"Shoot!" cried the crowd.

With great care, Spider drew back his foot and chipped the ball ... just over the bar, exactly as his captain had done.

For a moment there was a shocked silence. The players of both sides stood stock-still, boggle-eyed. The crowd lost its voice. Mr Smithers, who had been about to blow for a goal, nearly swallowed his whistle.

Then everyone started to shout at once. Darren Kelly yelped and threw himself backwards into the mud. Jason Best rushed up to Spider and pushed his finger into his chest.

"You useless idiot, Spider," he said. "What were you thinking of?"

"I was trying to do what you did," Spider said unhappily. "I'm sorry."

"Sorry?" said his captain fiercely. "You've just lost us the championship." He sent Spider off to the wing, where he'd be out of the way.

 # CHAPTER 6

The game was almost over. Standing out near the touchline, all by himself, Spider was a pitiful sight. He was muddy from head to toe, his shirt hung out of his shorts, his socks drooped round his ankles, his black hair was a spiky mess. He looked like he was about to burst into tears.

Parkfield mounted one last attack. Zoe Cole ran into the penalty area and shot; the Stoneley goalkeeper pushed the ball round the post.

"Corner kick," said Mr Smithers.
He kicked the ball towards Spider.

"Take it, Spider," called Darren Kelly.

Spider stumbled over to the corner flag. But as he stepped back to take the kick, his mind wandered. It wandered so far that his whole head felt empty.

Mr Smithers blew his whistle. The crowd shouted. His team-mates waved and shrieked. But Spider looked as if he had turned to stone.

Then he caught sight of someone in the crowd. It was his mum! Her face was bright red and she was puffing. She waved to Spider.

In an instant, Spider's mind slid back into place.

"Swing it in, Spider!" Jason Best screamed.

Spider remembered the afternoon before and that amazing banana kick. He saw in his mind the ball hitting that flowerpot ... With a spring, he ran forward and kicked across the ball with the top of his right foot.

The ball soared across the pitch towards the Stoneley penalty area. The Parkfield crowd groaned as the ball went away from the Stoneley goal.

But then it happened! The ball started to swerve.
It curved back in towards the Stoneley goal. The crowd
roared. Too late, the Stoneley goalkeeper saw the danger
and threw himself to his left. But the dipping ball passed
his fingertips and flew into the net.

Spider had scored!

The Parkfield crowd went wild. No one heard Mr Smithers
blow his whistle for the end of the match. Parkfield had
equalized with the very last
kick. It was a draw and
Parkfield, not Stoneley,
were champions.

Parkfield	Stoneley
1	1

The Parkfield players were over the moon. They jumped
in the air, they shouted, they danced and hugged each
other. Then they lifted Spider up on their shoulders and
carried him off the field.

"Well done, Spider," said Mr Smithers. "Well done! I knew you could do it." Then he turned to Spider's mum. "That boy's got great potential, Mrs McDrew," he said.

Spider's mum beamed. Then she planted a big kiss on Spider's muddy forehead.

"I got here just in time," she said. "You are clever, Spider."

Spider looked puzzled. "Did we win, then?" he asked.

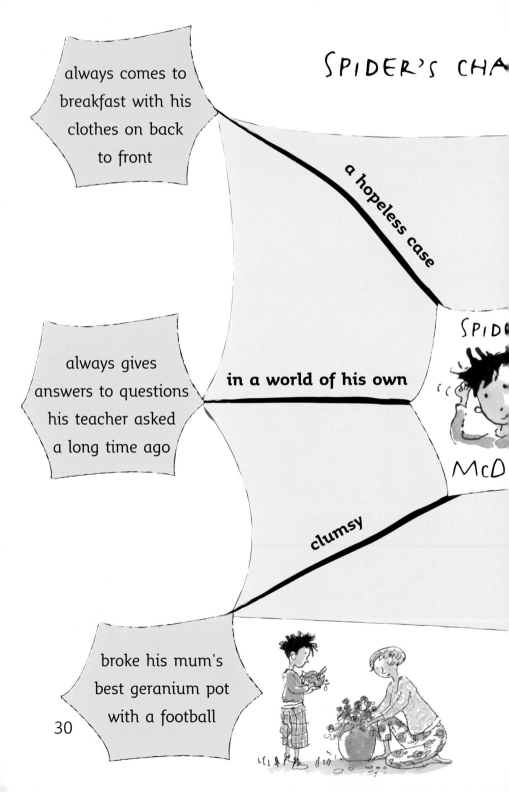

always comes to breakfast with his clothes on back to front

a hopeless case

always gives answers to questions his teacher asked a long time ago

in a world of his own

SPID

McD

clumsy

broke his mum's best geranium pot with a football

30

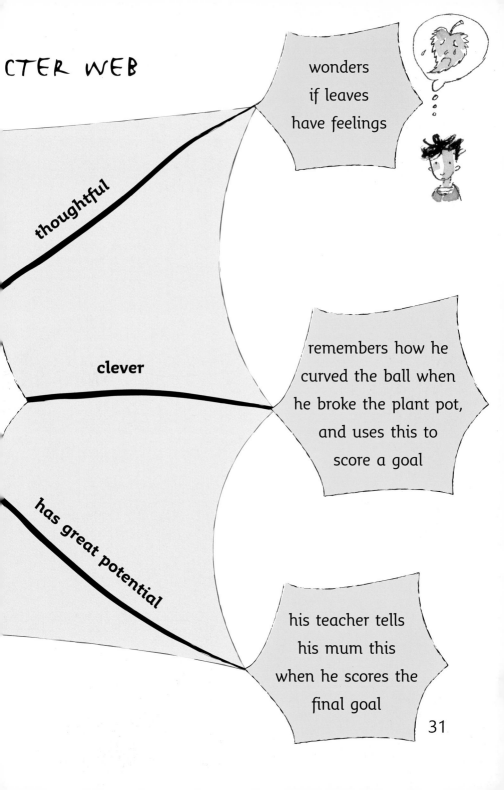

wonders
if leaves
have feelings

thoughtful

clever

remembers how he
curved the ball when
he broke the plant pot,
and uses this to
score a goal

has great potential

his teacher tells
his mum this
when he scores the
final goal

31

Ideas for guided reading

Learning objectives: tell main points of the story; refer to significant aspects of the text, e.g. opening, build up, and know how language is used to create these; discuss character by referring to the text and making judgements; investigate and reflect on feelings, behaviour and relationships; use drama strategies to explore stories

Curriculum links: ICT: combining text and graphics; PSHE: developing good relationships

Interest words: daydreaming, nickname, chickenpox, geranium, feelings, determination, equalised

Resources: computer

Getting started

This book can be read over two guided reading sessions.

- Read the front and back covers together. Ask the children to discuss what the story will be about. Have they come across Spider McDrew before? (Some children will recognise Spider from the Collins Big Cat book *Spider McDrew and the Egyptians*).

- Look at the pictures of Spider. Ask the children to discuss why he is called Spider.

- List some adjectives that describe Spider's character based on their ideas.

Reading and responding

- Model reading p2 of the story to children using appropriate expression and voices.

- Dwell on Spider's mum's phrase: "Oh, Spider, you're a hopeless case." Ask the children what this means.

- Ask them to look at the picture and find evidence that Spider is a 'hopeless case'. How do they think he feels when he's called this?

- Read aloud, in pairs, to the end of the chapter. Encourage reading with appropriate expression.